Echo and the Bat Pack

TREASURE IN THE GRAVEYARD

text by Roberto Pavanello
translated by Marco Zeni

STONE ARCH BOOKS
a capstone imprint

First published in the United States in 2012
by Stone Arch Books
A Capstone Imprint
1710 Roe Crest Drive
North Mankato. MN 56003
www.capstonepub.com

Text by Roberto Pavanello
Original cover and Illustrations by Blasco Pisapia and Pamela Brughera
Graphic Project by Laura Zuccotti and Gioia Giunchi

© 2006 Edizioni Piemme S.p.A., via Tiziano 32 - 20145 Milano- Italy
International Rights © Atlantyca S.p.A., via Leopardi, 8 — 20123 Milano, Italy —
foreignrights@atlantyca.it

Original Title: IL TESORO DEL CIMITERO

Translation by: Marco Zeni

www.batpat.it

LIbrary of Congress Cataloging-in-Publication Data is available on the Library of Congress
website.

ISBN: 978-1-4342-4248-8 (hardcover)
ISBN: 978-1-4342-2249-7 (library binding)

Summary: Echo needs his new friends to help him uncover who's been searching for treasure
in the cemetery.

Designer: Emily Harris

Printed in China
0412/CA21200581
042012   006679

TABLE OF CONTENTS

HELLO THERE!

I'm your friend Echo, here to tell you about one of the Bat Pack's adventures!

Do you know what I do for a living? I'm a writer, and scary stories are my specialty. Creepy stories about witches, ghosts, and graveyards. But I'll tell you a secret — I am a real scaredy-bat!

First of all, let me introduce you to the Bat Pack. These are my friends. . . .

Becca

Age: 10

Loves all animals (including crocodiles, bats, and even ravens)

Excellent at bandaging broken wings

Michael

Age: 12

Smart, thoughtful, and good at solving problems

Doesn't take no for an answer

Tyler

Age: 11

Computer genius

Funny and adventurous, but scared of his own shadow

Dear fans of scary stories,

Have you ever wondered what the quietest place in the world is? You might think it's a mountain forest, or the African desert, or maybe your attic. Sure, those are all quiet places, but let me tell you, there is no place quieter than a good old . . . cemetery!

Despite what you might have heard, cemeteries, especially abandoned ones, are quiet, peaceful places. They're places where nothing weird ever happens and where no one would ever disturb you, especially at night. That's why I have always lived inside a crypt in an abandoned cemetery.

In fact, that's where this story begins. It begins before I even met my Bat Pack friends. One night, I was busy working away in my crypt. You see, writers need plenty of privacy, and my crypt is the perfect place to hide away and write. At least that's what I thought, until that night, when I witnessed something very strange indeed. . . .

Chapter 1

Run, Bat, Run!

It was the dead of night. I had been staring at a blank page for hours. I had my quill in my hand, my inkwell close by, and not a single idea for my next story. That can happen to writers sometimes, you know. Writer's block. I decided to go get some fresh air and hopefully find some inspiration.

I left my crypt and took flight. The night was awesome! The sky was cool and clear — not a cloud in sight. It was the perfect time for a little night flight. I flew over the cemetery a couple of times. While I was there, I decided to grab a mouthful of fruit flies. Unless you're a bat you can't begin to imagine how much I love fruit flies. They are delicious!

After I was finished with my snack, I hung upside down from the branch of an old oak tree close to the cemetery wall. Letting all the blood rush to your head is bad for humans, but it gives us bats lots of good ideas. The sky was upside down from where I hung, but it was beautiful.

It looked like a big black cloak dotted with beautiful, shining pearls. Boy, what a poetic sentence! My creativity was clearly starting to come back.

I closed my eyes and listened to the noises of the night with my amazing bat hearing. The light whispering of the wind ruffling the tree leaves, the chirping of a night-loving cricket, the rustling of snakes among the headstones. Then, all of a sudden, everything was silent. I kept dangling upside down from the tree branch until, out of the blue, a terrible creaking sound sent a chill down my spine. Someone was opening the old cemetery gate!

Who was that? My little brain put two and two together. I only had two options: I could freeze there and pretend I was a leaf, or plunge headfirst toward the mystery — and danger! You shouldn't be surprised to hear that I chose the first option.

A stooping, hooded figure emerged from the mist. The man was cloaked in a long black cape. He carried an old burlap sack over his shoulder.

He stopped in front of a tombstone that was slightly larger than all the others. Two long, skinny, bone-white hands opened the burlap sack and pulled out a pickax. He pushed the flat end of the tool under the edge of the tombstone and used it as a lever.

The man kept his back to me, but I could see his body shake with effort as he tried to lift the heavy stone slab. Eventually, he managed to open a passage about three feet wide. He dropped the pickax and took two steps back, panting for breath. Then he raised his eyes to the sky and let out a loud, high-pitched cry: *Kraaaaaa! Kraaaaaa!*

Moments later, a black raven emerged from the darkness. It flew silently through the night sky and came to rest on the nearest tombstone.

"Did you find it?" the hooded man asked.

The raven shook its head and fluttered its wings, as if to say no. The man clenched his fists in rage.

I was starting to feel very nervous. I wanted to fly away, but I couldn't even find the courage to take a breath. I was too afraid that they would realize I was there.

As I watched, the hooded figure neared the grave once again and descended into it through the passage he had created. I couldn't see what was happening down there, but based on the booming noises I heard, I could tell he was searching for something.

Finally, the figure emerged, empty-handed, from the grave. He raised his head in my direction, and I finally got a good look at him. His face was a hollow white skull!

I was so scared of his terrifying face that I let out a whimper of fear. That was my one mistake. It was just a tiny little squeak, I swear, but he heard it anyway.

With his body still half in the grave, the man stretched his arm toward me and pointed with one of his long, bony fingers. He showed his ugly bird right where I was hanging. It didn't take a rocket scientist to realize that he meant,

"Get that spy. Dead or alive!" As expected, the raven darted in my direction.

My little brain put two and two together again. This time I concluded that I only had one option. Scram!

Chapter 2

Daring Stunts

Before I go any further, I should tell you how I became friends with the Silver kids, my Bat Pack, and how we all ended up together in the same terrifying adventure.

Fogville's bell tower had just struck three, and Michael Silver was still wide awake. He'd been tossing and turning for hours, trying to fall asleep. He tried to concentrate on something relaxing, like a beach vacation, for example. But all he could think about was the time he'd been stung by a jellyfish.

So much for relaxing, Michael thought.

Michael glanced across the room to where his younger brother Tyler slept. Tyler's feet stuck out from under the covers, and his head was buried beneath a pillow. He'd been sound asleep for hours. He was snoring like a bear.

Michael sighed and decided to read for a little while. *Maybe that will make me tired*, he thought. He reached over to his bedside table to turn on his light and grab his glasses. As soon as he put the glasses on his face, however, the lenses fogged.

"Uh-oh," Michael muttered. "That's a bad sign." As I was about to learn, whenever Michael's glasses fogged, it meant trouble was on the way.

Michael wiped his glasses clean and picked up his favorite book, *Tales of Terror* by Edgar Allan Poultry, from the table next to his bed. Michael loved scary stories, and Poultry was the only writer who could send chills down his spine.

He'd just started reading when the bedroom door flew open. His younger sister, Rebecca — Becca for short — burst into the room. "Something's about to happen," she announced. "I can feel it!"

Michael looked up from his book. Becca's green eyes were worried as she stared back at him. Michael knew that if Becca was worried, it had to be serious. She was never wrong.

She pointed at something outside the window. "Look, down there!" she shouted. Tyler woke up with a start and fell off the bed, pulling half the covers off with him.

"What the heck is going on?" he asked, sounding half-asleep and confused. "What are you yelling about?"

"Shhh!" warned Becca. "Can you hear that? Whatever it is, it's getting closer. . . ."

The three of them stood there and listened. In the distance, they could hear piercing shrieks and faint, hoarse birdcalls.

"It sounds like an owl with a sore throat chasing a scared mouse," said Tyler.

His sister ignored him and walked over to the window. Michael put down his book and followed her.

"Look, there they are!" Becca cried, pointing

out the window. She had finally spotted me. I was flapping my little wings like crazy, trying to get rid of the raven who was still chasing after me. His *kraaa-kraaas* echoed menacingly in my ears. I knew he was saying, "I'll get you! I'll get you!"

"Look, it's a bat!" cried Becca. "That big black bird is chasing it!"

"Quick, Tyler, turn on the light!" Michael said. "Becca, open the window!"

"Already done," she answered.

"What exactly are you planning to do?" Tyler asked.

"I'm going to get him to come in here," Michael answered, rummaging frantically through a drawer. "I just need to find . . . there it is!" he said, raising a small metal object triumphantly.

"What's that?" Tyler asked, walking over to join his brother and sister at the window.

"It's an ultrasound whistle," Michael explained. "You use it for dogs, but I bet we can use it to save that poor bat. Bats can hear ultrasound too." He put the whistle to his lips and gently blew. It didn't make a sound.

"It's not working," Tyler complained. "I don't hear anything."

But to my desperate ears, that was the sound of salvation! I realized that it was coming from an open window, and I flew in its direction at full speed.

"Becca! Tyler! Grab one of the shutters, and close the window as soon as I tell you to!" Michael said. "Ready?"

"Ready!" Becca replied.

"Almost ready," said Tyler, looking for one of his slippers.

"Come on, Tyler, hurry up!" Michael hollered. "It's almost time!"

As I got closer, I could see three kids standing on the other side of the window. They were all waving at me, trying to signal me to fly faster. I wanted to tell them that I was flying as fast as I could! And even though my little wings were rotating as fast as the blades of a blender, the

raven had almost caught me. I knew I was done for!

Suddenly I thought of a move I'd learned from my cousin, Limp Wing. He was on an aerobatic display team. The move was called the "Death Loop."

I was not really in the mood for "looping." (Maybe I forgot to mention that I'm afraid of heights.) But I definitely wasn't in the mood to be caught by that ugly raven! So I closed my eyes, crossed my toes (my fingers were busy),

counted to three, and . . . zoom! Bringing my wings close to my body, I made a perfect loop in the pitch-black sky. It was so graceful that I almost gave myself a round of applause.

Caught by surprise, the raven swung left and right like a sparrow on his first flying lesson. By the time he figured out where I'd gone, I had a 30-foot lead on him. I zeroed in on the window and shot through it like a cannon ball. Well, maybe more like a tennis ball.

As I flew in the open window, Michael cried, "Now!" Becca and Tyler immediately closed the window. I managed to squeeze through, but the raven didn't. He smacked against the window with a loud *SPLAT!* Amazingly, the glass didn't shatter. In fact, the raven came out of the collision without a scratch. He started circling the house, squawking threateningly.

"Shoo! Go away, you ugly bird!" Tyler said, waving his t-shirt in front of the window.

"Don't worry, Tyler," Becca said. "I'll deal with it."

Becca stared hard into the bird's eyes as it hovered in front of the window. A few seconds later, the raven turned around and plunged back into the dark night.

To tell you the truth, I didn't see all of that personally. It was all a matter of braking, you see. I was flying so fast that once I was inside, I couldn't avoid the wall in front of me. I smacked right into it! So much for my flying expertise. But hey, I did the best I could — I'd like to see you do better!

Luckily, I bounced off the wall and onto a soft mattress. But, since I had already passed out, I didn't realize that either.

Chapter 3

The Silver Kids

When I woke up, I saw three pairs of eyes staring down at me. I tried to move, but I hurt all over. Then I remembered what had just happened, and a chill ran down my little wings. Those three kids had saved my life!

"Hey there," the girl said. She had long red hair, freckles, and green eyes. She looked worried as she stared down at me. "We thought you were a goner. I'm Becca."

"I'm Michael," said the older-looking boy. He was wearing glasses and had dark, neatly combed hair. His pajamas were so neat it seemed like they'd been ironed. I couldn't believe he was so put-together in the middle of the night.

"Hi! I'm Tyler," said the third one. He was chewing on something. His hair was messy, and his shirt was wrinkled. It looked like he'd just rolled out of bed. When you think about it, I guess he had.

"That was a close call, wasn't it?" said Becca. She picked me up and cradled me in her arms.

"One more second and you would have been that raven's dinner!" Michael added.

I was just about to speak up when a terrible pain shot through my right wing. I must have broken it. Before I could complain, Becca was bandaging my wing. She did a better job than a doctor would have.

Where did she learn to bandage a wing so well? I wondered.

When she was finished fixing my wing, Becca laid me gently on a pillow on one of the beds. "We should give him a name," she said, sitting down next to me. "How about Batty?"

"I don't like it. He looks like a rat. How about Ratty?" Tyler said.

"How about Napoleon?" Michael suggested.

"I already have a name!" I said.

All three stared at me. From the looks on their faces, I realized that they hadn't seen that one coming!

"You . . . you can *talk*?" Michael stuttered.

"Of course," I said.

"Wow!" gasped Becca.

"Cool!" cried Tyler. "Where did you learn to talk?"

"I lived in a library for years," I explained. "In the afternoon, the librarian would read stories to children. He was very good! I would hide and listen. So, little by little . . ."

"Wow, a talking, flying rat!" Tyler exclaimed. "What's your name?"

"It's Echo, and for your information, I am not a rat. I am a bat," I informed him. "A very grateful bat. You three saved my life!"

Once they knew I could talk, the kids wanted to know everything about me. Becca gathered information on my nightlife, and Michael asked questions about my "house" at the old cemetery. The only thing that Tyler seemed to care about was whether I just ate fruit bugs or if I liked pizza, too.

The hardest thing was convincing them that I could not only talk, but that thanks to the old librarian, I could write as well. (I'm a pretty good mystery writer, if I do say so myself.)

"A writing rat? Um, sorry, I mean, a writing bat," Tyler said, still sounding shocked. "Wow!"

Becca was still concerned about the raven. "Why was that raven following you? Did you make him mad?" she asked me, looking worried.

"No!" I exclaimed. "He's the one who made *me* mad! Him and his terrible master."

"Terrible master?" Michael repeated. "What do you mean?"

"Are you sure you want to hear this?" I asked. "I don't want to scare you."

"We don't get scared that easily," Becca insisted. "Tell us the story."

So I told them about the hooded skeleton, the dug-up grave, and the ugly black bird that had appeared out of nowhere and tried to eat me.

"Well, don't worry about it now, Echo," Tyler said. "You're safe here."

"You can stay here as long as you want," Michael added.

"At least until your wing is okay," Becca said with a smile.

"And then?" I asked shyly.

"Then you can go back to your home in the cemetery," Michael said.

"By myself?" I asked. I didn't like the sound of that.

"Don't tell me you're afraid!" Michael said.

"To tell you the truth, I am scared wingless at the thought of running into that terrifying skeleton again!" I admitted.

The children exchanged a silent glance, and then Michael spoke. "Then we'll take you back when you're ready," he promised. "Would that make you feel better?"

"A little bit," I said. "But I think you're all crazy for offering."

"You know, Echo, you're not the first one to tell us that," Tyler said.

Chapter 4

Family Breakfast

The next morning, I was startled awake by a high-pitched female voice yelling, "Breakfast!"

"We're coming, Mom!" Becca hollered back. Michael was busy brushing his hair, and Tyler was struggling with a sweater that he had put on inside out.

"It might be a good idea if you don't talk for now," Becca reminded me as she carried me down the stairs. "At least at first. I don't want my parents to freak out."

"Don't worry, I'll be quiet as a mouse!" I answered.

Becca walked into the kitchen, followed by her brothers. A man with a mustache sat at the table reading the newspaper. A woman with the same red hair as Becca stood at the stove cooking. I figured the adults must be Mr. and Mrs. Silver, the parents of my three new friends.

"What was all the noise I heard last night?" Mr. Silver asked, glancing over his newspaper. Then he noticed me. "Oh no, Becca, another animal? Didn't we agree that there would be no more —"

"Oh, George," Mrs. Silver interrupted him, "it's just a scared little bat. Look at how cute he is!"

"Well, he sure is, but I hoped that the baby crocodile would be the last pet," Mr. Silver replied. "You thought he was cute, too, and he almost bit my foot off, remember?"

"But this is just a bat!" Becca replied. "He was being chased by a raven, and if we hadn't let him in, he would have been killed. He even broke a wing when he landed, see? I had to bandage it. We can't let him go. He's hurt."

"Please, Dad?" Michael added. "Can we keep him, just for a little while?"

Mr. Silver sighed. He knew when he was outnumbered. "Oh, all right," he said. "Just until his wing is healed."

The kids turned happily to their breakfast. Tyler appeared to be the happiest, at least judging by the size of his cheeks, which were as full as a hamster's.

"Have you seen the news this morning?" Mr. Silver asked, pointing at the paper with

his coffee mug. "A prisoner broke out from the Black Gate Penitentiary last night."

"Goodness!" exclaimed Mrs. Silver, who was busy making more eggs and bacon for Tyler. "Who was it?"

"Some man named Victor Mancino," Mr. Silver replied. "According to this, he's a very dangerous robber. Ten years ago he and his partner were arrested during a bank robbery."

"I don't think it's a good idea for us to go to school with a criminal like that on the loose," Tyler said. He frowned. "We could be kidnapped!"

"Kidnapping you wouldn't be a very good idea, Tyler," his mother said with a laugh. "You eat too much! Hurry up, the school bus is coming."

Chapter 5

The Raven Again

After breakfast, the kids went to school, Mr. Silver went to work, and Mrs. Silver went grocery shopping. For a while, I wandered around the empty house. I was feeling very sleepy. Bats are not particularly active during the day, you know. As a matter of fact, we sleep like logs. So I went back to the children's room to find a spot where I could curl up and take a nap.

I was just getting comfortable when a black shadow flew past me outside the window.

The raven! He must have seen me, because he abruptly changed his direction and headed back toward the house. I squatted against the wall, shaking like a leaf. He landed on the windowsill, right above me. I was trembling with fear, and on top of that, one of my wings didn't work! Luckily, the windows were closed, but I could still hear his voice — and I didn't like it one bit.

"I'll get you sooner or later," he said. "I'll get you!" Then the raven flew away.

Trying my best to stay hidden, I peeked out the window. As I watched, the raven flew from house to house. He was peering through the windows, like he was looking for something.

Once he was finally out of sight, I went to Becca's bed and fell asleep. Sometimes I have the most wonderful dreams during the day. Unfortunately, they can be a tad . . . well, let's say . . . dangerous.

That particular day I dreamt I was standing on a branch. Next to me was a little crow I was teaching to fly. I had just opened my wings and was about to jump off the branch when I felt someone grab me and yell, "Stop, Echo! Don't do it!"

I opened my eyes and realized that I was standing on the edge of the stairwell. I'd been about to leap off! A hand was gripping me tightly around my middle. Luckily, Becca had grabbed me just in time to save me from splattering on the floor!

I felt dizzy. How on earth did I get there?

"You must have been having a bad dream, Echo!" she said. "But that's no reason to leap into the air with a broken wing!"

When her brothers came home, I told them that I had seen that evil bird again and that I thought he had been looking for something.

"We have to keep our eyes peeled," Michael said thoughtfully. "I don't know what that bird is looking for, but something doesn't add up."

The following day at breakfast, Mr. Silver gave us an interesting clue. "Did you hear what happened last night?" he asked, showing us the newspaper. "Someone tried to break into the Newtons'. Mrs. Newton said that she heard some suspicious noises coming first from the roof and then from the chimney. But when she went into the living room, all she could find was black soot scattered all over the place. The burglars had already left, but they hadn't taken anything. Isn't that strange?"

It was strange, all right. The four of us exchanged an uneasy look, but no one said anything.

I stayed at home during the day and kept my eyes peeled all week, even when I was falling asleep on my feet.

Every afternoon at the same time, I saw the raven fly over Fogville, peering in windows for whatever it was he was looking for. Every

morning, Mr. Silver would read the newspaper. It was always the same story about an attempted burglary. The details never changed: noises coming from the roof and the chimney, black soot spread all over the living room, and nothing missing. No trace of the burglars.

Chapter 6

Mrs. Trump's Bedroom

On Saturday evening, Becca, Michael, Tyler, and I were all sitting around the Silver family's living room, trying to make sense of the mystery. There hadn't been any breaks in the case. Suddenly we heard someone screaming for help. It sounded like it was coming from the house next door.

Becca quickly put me in her pocket as we all ran next door to Mrs. Trump's house. Mr. and Mrs. Silver followed closely behind.

Once inside, we found Mrs. Trump sitting in a chair in the living room, holding a broom and breathing heavily.

She was staring, wide-eyed, at the mess left by the burglars. The room was a disaster. There was black soot everywhere, chairs were knocked over, vases were smashed, and the window was wide open.

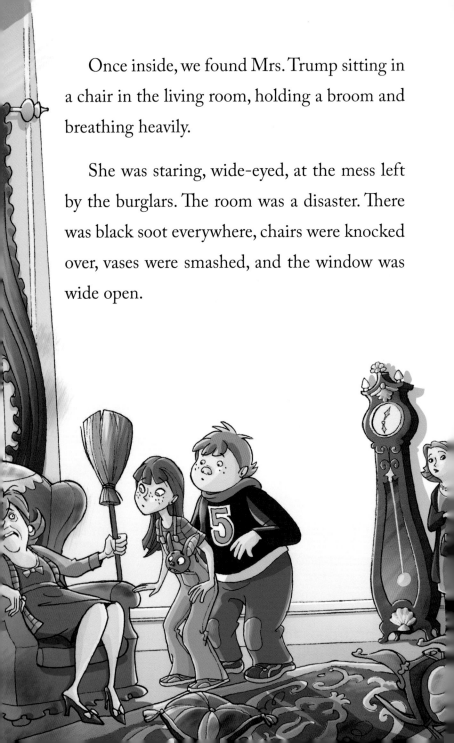

"Look at this place!" said Mr. Silver. "Are you okay, Petunia?"

"I'm fine, I'm fine . . ." the woman answered in a shaky voice.

Michael took out a magnifying glass and started poking around.

"It's all over now," Mr. Silver said. "Don't worry. We'll call the police."

Tyler tried to be helpful by sticking his head in the chimney. When he pulled it back out, his face was covered with black soot.

"The police won't be able to help," Mrs. Trump said with a sigh. "They can't do anything to hunt down ghosts."

"Ghosts?" Mr. Silver repeated. "What ghosts? What are you talking about?"

"I saw him, George! I saw him with my own eyes!" Mrs. Trump insisted. "He wears a black hooded cape, and his face is white, and he walks on rooftops."

"There's no such thing as ghosts, Petunia," Mrs. Silver said, patting the woman's shoulder. "You're just in shock."

"I'm telling you I saw him!" Mrs. Trump insisted. "There was someone else with him, too. Someone with two big wings as black as night. He came out of a dark cloud and tried to grab me, but I fought back with this," she said, waving her broom in the air.

I don't know why, but Mrs. Trump's last words caught me by surprise. I abruptly raised my head out of Becca's pocket and came face to face with Mrs. Trump. The poor woman screamed in sheer terror.

"Another one! Another one!" she cried, throwing a shoe at me. "Get him out of here! Get him out of here!" Luckily, she had very bad aim and missed me.

"Calm down, Petunia," Mr. Silver said. "It's just a little bat. He's one of my daughter's pets. There's nothing to be afraid of."

Mr. and Mrs. Silver eventually managed to calm down Mrs. Trump. The four of us were still in the living room, waiting for the police to come, when Michael picked up something off the floor. "Psst," he whispered. "Take a look at this!"

Becca and Tyler walked over. Michael held out what he'd found. It was a long black feather. A raven's feather.

Chapter 7

Black Riding Hood

The police didn't find any evidence in Mrs. Trump's house. No fingerprints, no footprints, nothing. All they could say was that nothing had been stolen. The lack of evidence almost made it seem like the intruder *had* been a ghost.

Unfortunately, the story of the break-in didn't end there. Mrs. Trump was so worked up that she decided to call all the newspapers in town and tell reporters about the black-caped ghost and the mysterious black creature from the chimney. As a result, Fogville's newspapers came up with crazy headlines like:

"GHOST BURGLAR BREAKS INTO ELDERLY WOMAN'S HOUSE!"

"MYSTERIOUS CAPED CREATURE SEEN FLYING OVER TOWN'S ROOFTOPS!"

After the break-in at Mrs. Trump's house, the town was full of sightings of the ghost and his mysterious friend. People started going crazy. Some claimed that during the full moon they had seen the caped ghost riding a huge black bird over the streets of Fogville. Others swore that he could enter houses by walking through the walls, leaving behind clouds of soot on rugs and chairs when he fled.

In all that craziness, there was one bit of good news. My wing had healed, and I could finally fly again.

I couldn't imagine how much I would regret that soon.

One week after the break-in next door, the Silver kids came up to the attic, where I was allowed to hide out and sleep until sundown. It had become my new den.

"Echo, we've been talking," Becca said. "If we're going to solve this mystery, we need to learn more about this ghost."

"What do we know so far?" I asked.

"Well, it's obvious that the hooded man with the raven that you saw at the cemetery is the same guy that's been breaking into people's houses," Becca said.

"Yes," I said, "but who is he?"

"We can't rule out the possibility that he might really be a ghost," Michael suggested.

Tyler snorted and rolled his eyes at Michael's suggestion.

"I think he's just a regular burglar who likes to wear costumes," Becca said.

"Maybe he's Black Riding Hood bringing flowers to his grandma's grave," said Tyler, sprawling on the bed.

"Could you at least try to be serious for five minutes?" Becca snapped at him. Tyler just shrugged and pulled his baseball cap down over his eyes.

"There's only one way to figure out who he is," Michael said. He pushed his glasses back up his nose and looked at us one by one.

"Oh, no," Tyler said nervously, jumping up from the bed. "I know what you're thinking. We're not going to the cemetery! No way! Count me out!"

"Don't tell me you're scared!" Michael said.

"Of course I'm scared!" Tyler said. "It's a cemetery!"

"Okay, we'll put it to a vote," Michael said. "That's only fair. Whoever wants to find out what the hooded burglar looks like, please raise your hand."

Michael and Becca instantly shot their hands in the air. To tell you the truth, I was scared wingless at the idea of seeing that skeleton and his bird friend again. But I didn't want to let my friends down. I mustered up all my courage and raised my now-healed wing. Three against one.

"That settles it. Let's go!" Michael said.

Tyler glared at me.

"Didn't you say you wanted to see where I live?" I said, trying to be funny. Not surprisingly, Tyler didn't laugh.

"Grab your camera, Tyler," Michael said calmly. "And get a jacket, too. It gets cold in cemeteries at night."

Chapter 8

A Trip to the Graveyard

It was already dark when we left the Silvers' house and headed to the cemetery.

We walked silently in a single line. I led the way, since I was the only one who knew where we were going.

Michael was right behind me. He was wearing a miner's headlamp he'd found in the closet. The light on his helmet shone brightly — not that I needed it to see. Becca followed close behind her brother. Tyler, wearing his

usual backward baseball hat and a pair of bright orange sneakers, brought up the rear. He was still mad about being outnumbered and stomped along behind us.

"Could you possibly walk any quieter?" Becca asked. "We're trying to keep a low profile, you know."

Tyler just ignored her. When we finally got to the cemetery, the gate was still closed. That meant that the ghost wasn't there yet.

Michael pushed the gate open very carefully, but the rusty hinges still let out a loud creak. We all held our breath. It was eerily quiet.

"This way," I whispered, leading them quickly through the cemetery. The graves were surrounded by gray mist that reflected the moonlight.

What a beautiful place, I thought. *It's so*

peaceful. Too bad I was the only one who felt that way.

"There's my house, the crypt!" I said proudly, pointing to the small stone building.

"Nice place you have there, Echo," Tyler said sarcastically. "Can I borrow it for my Halloween party?"

"Cut it out, Tyler!" Michael said. "Do you think we could hide there while we wait, Echo?"

"Sure," I answered. "We'll be safe there. The side windows will give us a clear view of the cemetery, and we'll be out of sight."

As I said that, the gate creaked again, much louder than before. Our mysterious friend had arrived!

"I . . . I think we should go into the crypt now!" I suggested quickly. Michael, Becca, and Tyler must have agreed, because they were even faster than I was at getting inside.

Once inside, we all stood at the window of the crypt, our eyes glued to the cemetery's entrance. As we watched, the black shape of the hooded man appeared.

We all held our breath anxiously. Tyler was as pale as a ghost.

The man looked around suspiciously. Seeing no one, he turned his back on us and let out the same strange cry I'd heard him make the first time. *"Kraaaaaa! Kraaaaaa!"*

The raven was there in an instant.

"Did you find it?" the hooded man demanded.

The raven shook his head no and fluttered his feathers.

The man stomped his foot on the ground, picked up a stone, and threw it as hard as he could at the raven. The stone missed the bird by a hair.

"Hey!" protested Becca. "That's animal cruelty!"

Michael clamped his hand over her mouth.

Fortunately, the hooded man hadn't heard anything. He pulled a large pickax out of his bag and lifted one of the tombstones, revealing a hidden passageway underneath. He quickly disappeared inside. Ten minutes later, he reemerged empty-handed. Then he turned in our direction and proceeded to dig up another crumbling grave. The coffin was buried under so much dirt that the man had to use a shovel to remove it all.

He worked at it tirelessly, panting for breath, while the raven waited a few steps away, cheerfully picking at his feathers. After a while, the man emerged from the grave and flung the shovel away. He looked furious.

"What a temper," Tyler whispered. "He looks like Becca when she gets mad."

"That's not funny!" replied Becca, sticking out her tongue.

"Cut it out, you two!" said Michael briskly. "Tyler, hurry up and see if you can take a picture of him."

"Should I tell him to say 'cheese' before I shoot?" Tyler asked, fumbling with the camera.

"Just hurry up," Michael said. "Quick! Before he turns around."

Tyler held up the camera and pointed it at the hooded man. He looked through the viewfinder

to make sure he had the hooded figure at the grave in sight.

"Don't forget to turn off the fl—" Michael started to say.

But it was too late. Tyler had already pushed the button. The camera's flash went off, lighting up the cemetery, including the hooded man's face. And it gave away our hiding place! The man turned and looked right at us!

"Uh-oh!" Tyler gasped.

As soon as he'd recovered from his surprise, the man let out a terrifying growl and ran toward the crypt. The raven followed closely behind.

"This way, quick!" I whispered to the kids. I led them quickly to the dungeons beneath the crypt. Fortunately I knew them like the back of my wing.

We hurried down two flights of stairs until we ran into a huge stone wall blocking our way.

"We're trapped!" Becca gasped. "Now what do we do?"

"Step aside!" I said. I used my wing to push the eye of a little stone skull carved into the wall. The wall instantly spun around, and a huge cloud of moths flew up the stairs.

"Go in, quick!" I said. I pushed the skull's

eye a second time, and the wall slid closed
behind us. We were safe. When the hooded
man and his evil bird finally got there, all
they would find was a solid wall.

We each held our breath as we heard
the hooded figure approach the wall. He

and his raven searched, but they couldn't figure out where we'd gone. The kids and I all breathed sighs of relief when we finally heard them give up and leave.

Michael was the first one who dared to open his mouth. "Thanks, Echo," he said. "If it hadn't been for you . . ." He turned and glared at Tyler.

"You're welcome," I wheezed. "As my grandpa used to say, '*A wall ain't enough, if you've got the right stuff!*'"

Everyone looked confused. I didn't blame them. Grandpa's sayings didn't always make sense. Finally Tyler said, "Yeah, well . . . as long as the wall opens . . ."

"Do you think it's safe to go back now?" asked Becca. She looked around at the hundreds of white skulls that were staring at us from behind ancient rusty cages. "It's pretty grim in here."

"I'd like to get out of here too, " Michael added.

"See you, guys," Tyler said to the skeletons. "It's been a nice party, but it's definitely time for us to go now!"

We carefully walked back upstairs, listening for suspicious noises. We didn't hear anything. It seemed like the coast was clear.

"Maybe Black Riding Hood is finally gone," Tyler said. "Can we go back home now?"

But Michael didn't hear him. He'd walked over to the last grave the hooded man had dug up. He crouched down to take a better look at it.

"He's clearly trying to find something," Michael muttered. "But what? And what is the raven looking for?"

We all joined Michael at the open grave and

crouched down next to him, trying to answer those questions. Suddenly, we heard laughter. It froze the blood in our veins.

Chapter 9

Captain Trafalgar

"Well, well, well!" a voice said. "Looks like they finally sent the new recruits for the crew. Say, Nelson, ain't they a tad too young?"

Even though we were terrified, we managed to turn around. Before us stood the ghost of a hulking, bearded man. He was dressed like a sailor. He wore a large pirate's hat, a long jacket decorated with buttons, boots, and a sword in his belt. On his shoulder, the skeleton of a parrot rocked back and forth.

Becca and Michael huddled together. Tyler looked like he was going to faint, he was so scared. He quickly ducked behind his siblings to hide. As for me — well, I leaped into Becca's arms and closed my eyes.

"What's your name, son?" the ghost sailor asked.

"M-M-Michael, sir," Michael managed to say. "What's y-y-yours?"

"Captain Trafalgar, official of the fleet of Her Majesty, The Queen of England. And this is Admiral Nelson, my first mate," he said, pointing at the parrot. "Have you come to join up?"

"N-n-no, sir, actually . . . we . . . " Michael stuttered.

"NOOO?" bellowed the sailor. "YOU HAVE MADE ALL THIS RACKET!

YOU HAVE OPENED MY GRAVE AND UPSET MY SLEEP AND MY PEACE FOR NOTHING?"

At his angry tone, I disappeared back into Becca's pocket. Scaredy-bat indeed!

"It wasn't us, sir," Michael said quickly. "We just found out that someone's been digging up graves. He's looking for something, and when he can't find it he gets really angry. Do you have any idea who he might be?"

The ghost seemed to calm down a bit. He crossed his arms over his chest and turned to the parrot on his shoulder. "You reckon we can trust them, Nelson?" he asked.

The parrot swayed its head up and down in a nod.

"Very well," said the captain, leaning against his own tombstone. "You kids might as well make yourselves comfortable," he told us. "It's going to be a rather long story."

The Silver kids sat down to listen to his tale, while I curled up in the folds of Becca's sweater.

"Rumor has it that about ten years ago, a thief stashed a great deal of stolen money in one of these graves," Captain Trafalgar began. "This fellow drew a map of the cemetery showing which grave contained his loot, and then he hid the map away inside his chimney. Unfortunately, the thief died before he could retrieve the money, and he didn't tell anyone where he'd hidden the map!"

"That's what the raven is looking for in the chimneys!" Michael exclaimed. "He's looking for the map of the cemetery! Do you have any idea who the guy was?"

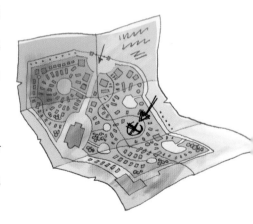

"Unfortunately not," the captain replied.

"How about which grave he buried the treasure in?" Becca asked hopefully.

"I don't know that either," the ghost said. "You see, the night that the money was buried, I had been invited to a navy ghost party. It was a huge celebration. Even Nelson was there!"

"You don't even know which chimney he hid the map in?" Michael asked.

"Son, do I look like the kind of man who goes around snooping in other people's chimneys? I would never risk ruining my beautiful uniform,"

Captain Trafalgar said. "Not even Nelson would do something of the sort."

"Could the hooded guy who opened your grave be the ghost of the thief? Maybe he came back to collect his money," Tyler suggested.

"As far as I know, ghosts don't use shovels," Becca said.

"Obviously someone else knew about the money," Michael said. "But who?"

We all stood quietly for a moment, thinking. The whole story made more sense now, but it was also much more complicated. No one had any answers.

"Well, I guess we should probably head home," Michael said finally.

"I agree," the captain said. "This cemetery ain't no place for kids."

"Thanks for the information, Captain. You've been very helpful," Michael said politely. "Is there anything we can do for you?"

"Well," the captain began. "There is one thing, actually. Come closer, son."

Michael moved closer to the ghost, who bent over and whispered something in his ear.

Michael nodded in agreement. "It's a deal!" he said. "Goodbye, Captain!"

"So long, sailors!" Captain Trafalgar called.

Becca, Michael, Tyler, and I headed back home, cold but satisfied. We tried to talk Michael into sharing what the ghost had told him, but he refused. He said that for the time being, it was a secret between the two of them.

"He seemed nice!" Tyler said. "I wasn't even that scared of him."

We all turned to stare at Tyler in disbelief. Michael, Becca, and I all burst out laughing. But then Michael asked me to do something. I stopped laughing pretty quickly after that.

Chapter 10

A Terrifying Face

You probably already guessed what Michael asked me to do, right? No? Well, I'll tell you. He had the nerve to ask me to look into all the chimneys in Fogville in search of the treasure map.

"No way!" I told him. There was no way I was risking getting caught by that raven. I was perfectly happy to hang out in the attic, thank you very much.

But Michael wouldn't take no for an answer. The next day, after school, he was at it again.

"Please, Echo!" he said. "We have to find the map before the raven does."

"Not in this lifetime!" I answered.

"How do we know this story about the treasure is even true?" Becca pointed out. "What if Captain Trafalgar made the whole thing up?"

"My point exactly," I agreed. "He looked crazy, talking to that parrot and all."

"Why would he have made it up?" Michael said. "Besides, the raven is searching the chimneys. Isn't that proof? We have to find out who the hooded man is and why he wants that money. Tyler, we need to see that picture."

"The picture? What picture?" his brother asked, raising his head from the comic book he was reading.

"The one we risked our life for in the cemetery," Michael said. "C'mon!"

"Oh, that one," Tyler said. "Give me a sec." He reluctantly set down his comic book and went to get his camera.

Tyler plugged the digital camera into the computer. A few moments later the screen came alive with a face so terrifying that we all jumped from our seats. A white skull was staring out at us, grinning in a not-exactly-friendly way.

"Ugh. He's even scarier than the first time I saw him," I said.

"Yes, but who is he?" Michael asked. "Does anyone have an idea?"

"I have an idea," Tyler said. "But let's have a snack first."

Even though it had nothing to do with solving the mystery, the idea of grabbing a snack helped distract us a bit.

Less than an hour later, Michael started again. "Listen, Echo," he said, "I know you're not exactly dying to go out there, but we need you. You're the only one who can get in and out of the chimneys during the day without anyone noticing."

"During the day?" I asked, bewildered. "How many times do I have to tell you that bats don't go out during the day? It's way too dangerous! I could fall asleep and get hurt. Do you want me to get hurt?"

"Of course not," Michael said. "But would you rather go at night with the raven and his master around?"

"No way!" I said. "But that bird flies around in the daytime, too. You know that."

"Yeah, but he doesn't go into the houses, so you'll be okay," Michael pointed out.

"But I'm scared!" I whimpered.

"Heroes get scared too," Michael said, "but they overcome their fear. That's how they become heroes."

He didn't know it, but Michael had struck the right chord. It's not that I really wanted to become a hero, but I suddenly heard a little voice inside of me saying, *C'mon Echo, find that map! You're the only one who can!*

Half an hour later, I was on my way to my destiny.

"Put these on. They'll protect you from the sun," Becca said, handing me a pair of blue sunglasses to wear. I put them on right away

and flew over to the mirror. *Hey, I looked pretty cool!* I thought. *Like a real tough guy!*

"Take this, too," Tyler said, putting his baseball hat on my head. "It's my good luck charm!"

I took one last look around to make sure that there were no sharp-beaked ravens lurking nearby. Then I set off on my mission.

You have no idea how narrow and dirty chimneys can be until you have to fly in one! The first time I went down one, I coughed for thirty minutes straight.

The second time, I got soot in my eyes, and the third time, I almost got stuck with my wing in the flue. On top of that, I almost ran into the raven, who was exploring the same area that day. I waited for him to disappear, and then I darted toward the Silvers' home. I was dirty, angry, and empty-handed!

"Tomorrow will be better!" Michael said.

"Tomorrow?" I repeated. I hoped I'd heard him wrong. "You mean I have to go back out there tomorrow, too?"

"Until we find the map, Echo. It's the only logical plan," Michael said.

I was about to tell him that it wasn't logical. It was

dangerous. But just then we heard Becca screaming downstairs.

We rushed to the living room and found her standing there, holding an old newspaper in her hands.

"What's going on?" Michael asked.

"Do you remember the prison escape Dad read about the other day?" she asked breathlessly. Her eyes were practically glued to the newspaper.

"Yes, the guy who escaped was . . . what's his name?" Michael asked. "Mancino! Victor Mancino!"

"Exactly," Becca replied. "We didn't get the whole story. Listen to what the article said. 'Many readers may remember that Victor Mancino gained notoriety under the nickname 'Victor Whiteskull' because of the strange mask that he used to wear when committing his crimes.'"

"A mask?" Tyler asked. "So what?"

"Not just a mask, Tyler," Becca said. "A skeleton mask!"

Chapter 11

A Computer Genius

This was the break we'd been waiting for! Excited, we hurried back upstairs.

"So the hooded figure who's been digging up graves in the old cemetery and terrorizing Fogville is the same man that escaped from Black Gate Penitentiary!" Michael said. "Victor Mancino, a.k.a. 'Whiteskull'!"

"Are you sure?" Tyler asked.

"It all makes sense," Michael said. "Captain

Trafalgar's story, the newspaper article, and especially the mask! It has to be him!"

"Couldn't it really be a ghost, just like people say?" I insisted, trying to rule out every other hypothesis.

"That's not a ghost!" Becca said, pointing at the ugly face that stared at us from the computer screen. "That's a real live criminal, and he's trying to get his hands on the money from his last job."

"But he's so lame that he doesn't even remember where he put it!" Tyler said, laughing.

"Not exactly," Michael said. "Remember what the captain said? The man who drew the map is dead, and he didn't tell anybody where he'd hidden it! The newspaper says that when Mancino was arrested for the bank robbery, he had an accomplice. The accomplice is the one who hid the money. Mancino probably trusted him."

"But that guy tricked him!" Tyler said.

"Maybe, but now we have to find the accomplice's name," said Michael. "Tyler, do you think you could do some research on this?"

"Are you kidding me?" his brother asked. "Piece of cake." He sat down at the computer, cracked his knuckles, and started typing at the speed of light.

"Wow!" I said. "You're really good!"

"Well despite how lazy he seems most of the time, Tyler is sort of a computer genius," Becca said.

She wasn't exaggerating. Five minutes later, we knew everything about the robbery, including the fact that despite the police investigation, the money was never recovered. We knew all

about the arrest of the two robbers and how the

mysterious accomplice had died in prison. Well,

he wasn't mysterious anymore. His name was

Max Lambert!

"We know he hid the map in his chimney,"
Michael said. "So now we just need to find out
where he lived. Tyler can you find his address?"

Tyler rolled his eyes. "Could you at least give
me a challenge?" he asked. He started typing

again, and a few seconds later, an address flashed on the screen:

13 Friday Street – Fogville.

We all stared at it in amazement. "But that doesn't make any sense," Becca stuttered. "That's *our* house!"

Chapter 12

Treasure Hunt

Everything happened so fast after that —
it's almost hard for me to remember! The kids
made me climb up the chimney in the living
room right away. I got all dirty and black with
soot, but sure enough, I found the map of the
stolen treasure hidden inside.

"I can't believe it!" Becca said, peering at the
map. "The guy who lived here before us was a
hardcore criminal."

"Do you think he hid anything else valuable in the house?" Tyler asked.

"Not now, Tyler," Michael said. "Come on, let's get going already. It's getting dark, and we have to get to the cemetery as soon as possible."

"The cemetery again?" Tyler grumbled. "Do we have to?"

"Absolutely!" his brother answered, taking a large package from one of his drawers. "How else are we going to catch Victor Mancino?"

"What's in there?" Becca asked.

"You'll find out soon," Michael told her.

Poor Tyler, I thought. I didn't want to go back to the cemetery either. But I was pretty sure Michael and Becca weren't going to take no for an answer.

Half an hour later, armed with a shovel and

a pickax, the Bat Pack was back at the cemetery. We walked quickly and quietly among the old graves. With a map to follow, finding the grave that held the treasure was a piece of cake.

"There it is!" Michael said, standing in front of a mound of earth with a small white tombstone. "All we have to do now is start digging."

Michael had just stuck the shovel into the ground when a piercing call carried over the night air. *Kraaaaaa! Kraaaaaa!*

I knew that sound all too well. It made the hair on the back of my neck rise!

We all whipped around. The hooded skull was staring at us, grinning menacingly. He was joined by his raven, who cawed, "We meet again, at last!"

"Look!" the man said. "They found our map for us. Wasn't that nice of them?" He reached

out one long, bony, white hand and slipped the map from Michael's hands.

"They even saved us the trouble of looking for the grave," the man continued. "They really are such nice kids. It's a shame that they've come to such a sticky end, isn't it?"

The Silver kids and I all huddled together, terrified. Actually, I had already slipped into Becca's pocket and put on my sunglasses, so that I couldn't see much of anything. But I was terrified nonetheless.

"You know, I've been watching you kids since the night you took a picture of me," the man told us. "You really thought I'd just let you go? All I had to do was follow you when you left the cemetery and keep an eye on you. It was easy! I was sure we'd meet again sooner or later."

Tyler picked that moment to try to act brave. "We know who you are!" he yelled. "We read it in the paper. You're Victor Mancino, the thief who escaped from prison! And that thing on your face is just a mask!"

"Bravo! That's correct!" the man said. "Unfortunately, none of you will ever be able to tell this story to anyone!"

With that, he grabbed Becca and pulled her toward him. She struggled to break free, but Mancino pinned her arms and slipped me out of her pocket!

"You'd better calm down if you want your

little friend here to stay in one piece," he warned angrily.

Becca froze. "Let go of him, you masked clown!" she yelled.

The man handed me over to his raven, who pinched me with his beak and flew off to the branch of a nearby tree. I was done for!

"Now," the masked criminal said to Tyler and Michael, "if you want your sister and your bat to be okay, START DIGGING!" he bellowed, pointing at the grave.

Tyler and Michael (well, mostly Michael) dug a pretty deep hole. They dug and dug until they hit something hard. Then they reached down and pulled a rusty, padlocked box from the earth.

As soon as Michael and Tyler handed the box to him, the man tore off the padlock and flung open the lid. He reached inside and started pulling out handfuls of money.

"My money!" he said, his voiced choked with emotion. "MY MONEY!"

Then, unfortunately, he remembered the four of us.

"And now, my dear friends, it's time for us to get down to business," he said. "It's nothing personal. But you four have seen way too much, so . . ."

He had just started to make his way toward the Silver kids when a deep voice roared from behind him, "SCARING KIDS LIKE THAT AIN'T FAIR. DON'T YOU AGREE, NELSON?"

We immediately recognized the voice. But Victor Mancino didn't. He turned around, and his jaw hit the ground.

In front of him stood the huge, ghostly figure of Captain Trafalgar. His skeleton parrot, Nelson, was balanced on his shoulder.

The captain glared at Mancino.

The raven gaped in surprise too. When Nelson flew toward him, the raven immediately took off, letting me go.

As soon as she saw that I was free, Becca stomped on Mancino's foot as hard as she could. While he was busy hopping in pain, Becca ran

toward Michael and Tyler. I flew back into her pocket to hide.

"Who are you?" whispered the hooded man, still clutching his sore foot.

The Captain didn't answer. Instead, he unsheathed his sword and started walking toward him. Mancino scurried backward until he bumped into a tree, and his mask fell off.

His real face was finally revealed. He looked skinny, pale, and extremely frightened.

"His hair is messier than mine!" Tyler said.

Seeing that the Captain was getting closer, Victor Mancino picked up the shovel we'd dropped and made a last-ditch attempt to escape.

"Take that!" he cried, swinging the shovel in front of him. "And that! And this!"

He was swinging that shovel pretty hard, I'll admit. He would have been a tough man for anyone to fight. But in this particular case, he was no match for his opponent. His blows passed harmlessly through the ghost of Captain Trafalgar. Finally realizing he wasn't making any progress, Mancino dropped the shovel and turned as white as a sheet.

"You're . . . you're . . . a g-g-ghost!" he cried. "A GHOST! HELP! SOMEBODY HELP ME! A GHOOOST!" He suddenly turned and fled. Screaming in terror, he vanished into the night.

"It's all over, kids," Captain Trafalgar said. "You can come closer now." The old sailor smiled.

"Thank you, Captain," Michael said. "You saved our lives!"

"We would have been goners if you hadn't shown up!" Becca agreed.

"Nonsense! Sailors help each other," answered the big man. "By the way, son, did you remember that, um . . . favor I asked of you?"

"Of course!" Michael said. "I have never been happier to do someone a favor!" And with that, he reached down and opened the big package he'd brought with him.

Chapter 13

Ghosts? Who Believes in Ghosts?

We snuck back home in the middle of the night, carrying the raven as a reminder of our adventure. Nelson, the ghost parrot, had managed to capture him, and we'd quickly returned to my crypt to lock him up in one of the cages we'd found.

We crept silently back into the house and went to bed. I was so tired that even though I'd never slept at night before, I went up to the attic, found a ceiling beam to hang from, and immediately fell asleep. It's just like Aunt Adelaide used to say. "If you sleep, it means you're tired!"

The first thing I heard the next morning was Mrs. Silver's high-pitched voice calling us down to breakfast. When we arrived at the breakfast table, we found eggs, bacon, orange juice, and pancakes waiting for us. *Life's pretty good here!* I thought.

* * *

Two days later, Mr. Silver read the news we'd all been waiting to hear from the *Fogville Echo*.

"Do you remember the robber who escaped from prison two weeks ago?" Mr. Silver asked.

"What robber?" Becca asked, playing dumb.

"You know, Victor Mancino," her father said. "It was in the paper. They found him near the old cemetery. Apparently he was crazy with fear.

He kept mumbling about running away from a ghost."

"Ghosts!" said Tyler, spreading honey on a piece of toast. "Do people actually believe that stuff?"

"That's not all, though," Mr. Silver continued. "Thanks to an anonymous call, the police found the money that Mancino and his partner had stolen during a bank robbery ten years ago. It was hidden in a garbage can."

"Huh," Michael said. "Imagine that."

* * *

In the following days, the sightings of the ghost thief and his black monster faded away. People's chimneys became quiet places once again, and Fogville returned to normal.

A week after we'd captured the raven, Becca asked me to go out into the woods with her. She wanted to set the bird free. Before she released him, she made him promise that from then on he would fly straight and never again hassle helpless bats. When he nodded in agreement, she opened the cage, and the bird flew off.

It might have been my imagination, but I thought I heard him say, "So long. We'll meet again, sooner or later."

And to this day, I don't know if he was saying goodbye or threatening me.

Chapter 14

No More Holes in My Soles

I'll bet you're still wondering what favor Captain Trafalgar had asked Michael. You have the right to be curious! After all, every good scary story needs a good ending.

Well, it turns out that when the old captain raised anchor and set sail from this world permanently (when he died, I mean), he had been doing pretty poorly financially. His crew found his dress uniform, which he'd hardly ever worn, to bury him in. Unfortunately, the same

couldn't be said for his shoes
— all he had was a pair of
knee-high black boots with
holes in their soles!

Poor Captain Trafalgar had never been able to get over the embarrassment of being buried in holey shoes. He claimed all the other sailors at the ghost parties teased him about it. So he asked Michael to find him a new pair of boots. After all the help the captain had given us, Michael had been more than happy to help.

All in all, it was quite the adventure! I can't say that my life was ever the same. I have new friends, my Bat Pack, and a new look — I wear sunglasses, sometimes a baseball cap, and even sneakers. What's more, I've moved!

Yep. Once the adventure was over, I thought long and hard about where I wanted to live. Did I want to go back to a cold, damp crypt, or would

I rather live in a warm, cozy attic with a nice family? It wasn't a difficult decision. So I moved in with the Silvers, and as soon as I'd recovered from all the commotion, I started writing scary stories again! Now that I had my Bat Pack, I knew there would be plenty more adventures and mysteries to come.

The last book I wrote? The one you just finished reading, of course!

An upside-down goodbye from your friend,

Echo

ABOUT THE AUTHOR

Roberto Pavanello is an accomplished children's author and teacher. He currently teaches Italian at a local middle school and is an expert in children's theatre. Pavanello has written many children's books, including *Dracula and the School of Vampires*, *Look I'm Calling the Shadow Man!*, and the Bat Pat series, which has been published in Spain, Belgium, Holland, Turkey, Brazil, Argentina, China, and now the United States as Echo and the Bat Pack. He is also the author of the Oscar & Co. series, as well as the Flambus Green books. Pavanello currently lives in Italy with his wife and three children.

CRYPT SWEET CRYPT

Scaredy-bat! I have to fly back to my crypt, but if I go the wrong way, I'll fly right into the hands of the skeleton ghost! Can you help me find my way back?

MIXED-UP MONSTERS

What a mess! Writing upside down sent a rush of blood to my head, and now all these monsters have mixed-up names. Can you unscramble the letters and find out who they are?

1. SNAENNFIETRK

2. MIERVPA

3. REWOFLEW

4. UMYMM

5. HTSGO

6. BMOIZE

7. EAS RENTSOM

THE MIDNIGHT
WITCHES

KING TUT'S
GRANDMOTHER

THE THING
IN THE SEWERS

Check out more
Mysteries and
Adventures with
Echo and the Bat Pack

TASTY CROSSWORD PUZZLE

What is my favorite food? Solve the crossword puzzle and the answer will appear in the yellow column!

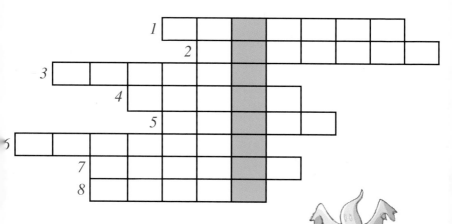

1. Scares the hooded man away
2. Escaped from Fogville's Penitentiary
3. Captain Trafalgar's parrot
4. When she's angry, you'd better stay away from her!
5. Where the treasure is hidden
6. What our group calls itself
7. The kids' last name
8. Michael gave these to Captain Trafalgar